Treaty 1915

THE MANUAL OF AERONAUTICS

THE MANUAL OF AERONAUTICS

AN ILLUSTRATED GUIDE TO THE LEVIATHAN SERIES

WRITTEN BY

MR. SCOTT WESTERFELD

ILLUSTRATED BY MR. KEITH THOMPSON

SIMON PULSE

NEW YORK   LONDON   TORONTO   SYDNEY   NEW DELHI

To Keith Thompson, whose art made this series far more amazing than I could ever have imagined, and to every author who ever started a novel with a map

SIMON PULSE
An imprint of Simon & Schuster Children's Publishing Division
1230 Avenue of the Americas, New York, NY 10020
First Simon Pulse hardcover edition August 2012
Copyright © 2012 by Scott Westerfeld
All rights reserved, including the right of reproduction
in whole or in part in any form.
SIMON PULSE and colophon are registered trademarks
of Simon & Schuster, Inc.
For information about special discounts for bulk purchases,
please contact Simon & Schuster Special Sales at 1-866-506-1949
or business@simonandschuster.com.
The Simon & Schuster Speakers Bureau can bring authors to your live event.
For more information or to book an event contact
the Simon & Schuster Speakers Bureau at 1-866-248-3049
or visit our website at www.simonspeakers.com.
Designed by Mike Rosamilia
The text of this book was set in Hoefler Text.
Manufactured in China
2 4 6 8 10 9 7 5 3 1
Library of Congress Cataloging-in-Publication Data
Westerfeld, Scott.
The manual of aeronautics : an illustrated guide to the
Leviathan series / written by Scott Westerfeld ; illustrated by Keith Thompson.
p. cm.
Summary: Illustrations and text provide detailed looks at the machines,
uniforms, creatures, and characters of the Leviathan book series.
ISBN 978-1-4169-7179-5 (hardcover)
[1. Space ships—Fiction. 2. Uniforms—Fiction. 3. Imaginary creatures—Fiction.
4. Science fiction.] I. Thompson, Keith, 1982– ill. II. Title.
PZ7.W5197
[Fic]—dc23
2011038924
ISBN 978-1-4424-5412-5 (eBook)

On the cover and page i: THE SULTAN'S AIRYACHT
The Ottoman sultan travels aboard his own airyacht, an opulent hot-air
balloon in the shape of a zeppelin. Driven by nine propeller shafts mounted
on mechanical arms, each of which can be controlled separately, the
airyacht requires a deft hand to control. But in the hands of an able pilot,
it can land as lightly as a feather among the crowded buildings of Istanbul.

Author's Note

The Leviathan trilogy was inspired by a set of century-old books I discovered on my parents' bookshelves as a child. These novels for teenagers had three main selling points: adventure, airships, and elaborate illustrations. At first I thought that airships and a dose of derring-do would be enough to recapture the magic of those crumbling old books. But then I ran across Keith Thompson's opulent artwork and realized that the Leviathan series could actually look like an adventure novel from 1914, illustrations and all.

Working with an artist was a new experience for me. Suddenly I had to know exactly what everything looked like. What were the precise dimensions of my fantastical machines? Did this stateroom have wallpaper? And what were the characters wearing at breakfast? A thousand details that one might overlook in a written scene had to be determined. A whole world had to be created from scraps of historical research and imagination.

Keith and I began to amass a set of "blueprints" to this world—deck plans for His Majesty's Airship *Leviathan*; cutaways of Alek's Stormwalker; uniforms and weapons for the soldiers of the British, German, Ottoman, Russian, and Austro-Hungarian armies. This necessary bit of world-building blossomed into its own book, a *Manual of Aeronautics* much like the one that Deryn carries in the novels.

The results are what you hold in your hands.

So here are the machines and creatures, the uniforms and characters of the Leviathan series, all in full color, posed and taken apart and labeled for your gratification. As a writer, I hope this demonstrates how much world-building goes into any work of alternate history or science fiction. As a geek, I hope you enjoy the deck plans.

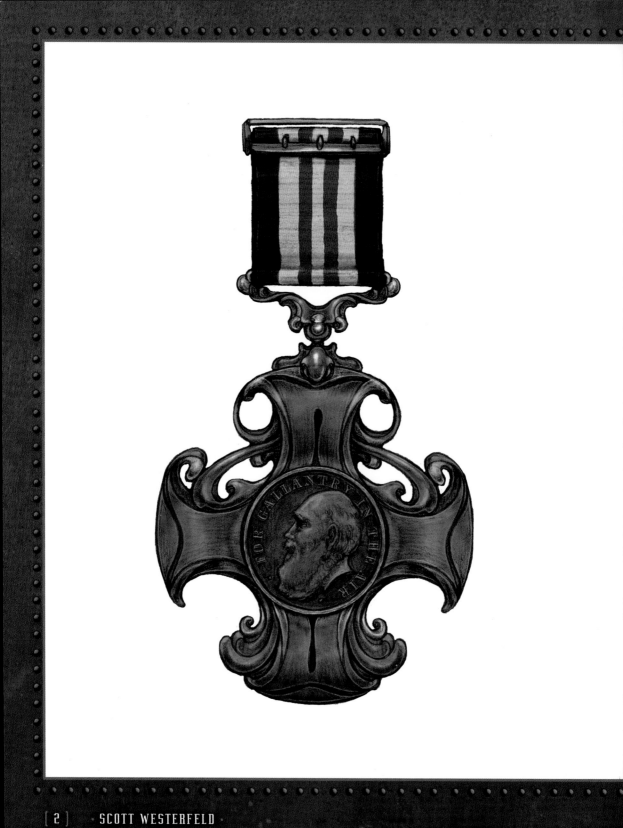

The medal bears the inscription "FOR GALLANTRY IN THE AIR"

The Darwinists

When Charles Darwin in 1854 first found in his microscope the "life threads" that make creatures evolve over time, he hardly realized that his discovery would break the world in two. Over the next sixty years the vast British Empire was built on the backs of living machines, inspiring many other nations to adopt the technological principles of Darwinism. As these countries traded and interbred fabricated beasts, the relationships among them grew stronger, finally becoming formal alliances. Led by Britain, France, and Russia, the Darwinist nations and their colonies spanned two-thirds of the world by 1914, and it seemed that their power would never be challenged. Of course, the Great War has proven such optimistic notions utterly wrong.

The *Leviathan*, Inside and Out

The *Leviathan* is a mix of machinery and beasts—a combination of flesh, muscle, steel, and fabricated wood. The huge airbeast is outfitted with a girdle of engines and crew spaces, and filled with an entire ecosystem of other creatures. Working together in fractious harmony, these elements make up one of humanity's greatest creations, the Darwinist airship.

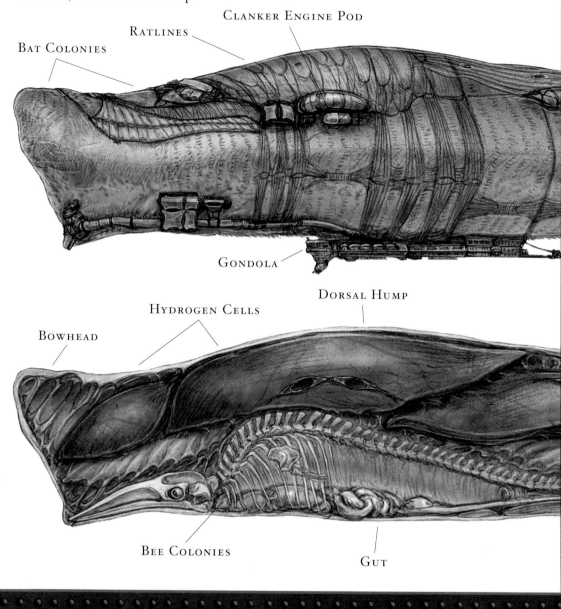

BAT COLONIES

RATLINES

CLANKER ENGINE POD

GONDOLA

BOWHEAD

HYDROGEN CELLS

DORSAL HUMP

BEE COLONIES

GUT

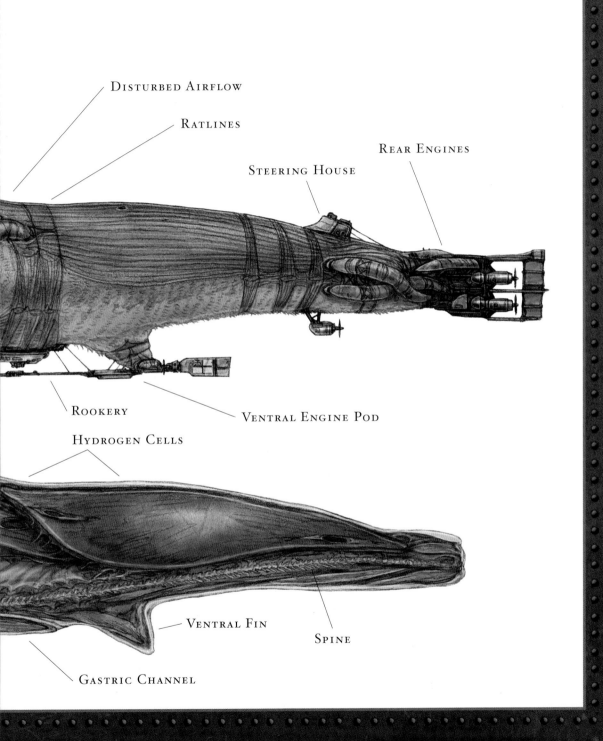

DISTURBED AIRFLOW

RATLINES

STEERING HOUSE

REAR ENGINES

ROOKERY

VENTRAL ENGINE POD

HYDROGEN CELLS

VENTRAL FIN

SPINE

GASTRIC CHANNEL

The Gondola

The gondola hangs from the belly of the airbeast, held on by a girdle of ratlines and other supports. Two hundred feet long, it is where most of the crew work and live, and where the airship's cargo and heavy weaponry are carried.

GALLEY

Here the ship's cooks prepare food for a hundred crewmen three times a day—breakfast before dawn, lunch at high noon, and dinner after the sun sets. They also make treats for rewarding the beasties. Message lizards, for example, are very fond of boiled rat.

CAPTAIN'S CABIN

OFFICERS' BATHS
Water is heavy, so is precious on any airship. Only officers are allowed to take showers or baths.

STOREROOMS
The lowest deck of the *Leviathan* is composed of storerooms and the cargo bay. Ammunition, medicine, and food for both men and beasties are stored here.

MIDDIES' MESS
This is where the midshipmen of the *Leviathan* take their meals. It is also used as a staff room for the officers, and for receiving guests on the ship. Officers take their meals in the captain's cabin together, or separately in their own cabins.

Gondola Cross-Section

ENGINE CONTROLS

On this control panel, receptors fabricated from cuttlefish skin are linked by nervous tissue to the engines' pods. Cuttlefish are able to change colors, so when colored paper is placed upon this control panel, the same color appears up in the pods. Red means "full speed ahead," purple means "half power," and blue means "quarter speed." Yellow means "full stop."

NAVIGATION ROOM

Here the navigators determine the best route to the ship's next destination, using sextant readings sent down from the spine of the airbeast, and landmark observations taken from the recon bell. Secret missions are planned here, and vital documents such as charts, codebooks, and orders from the Admiralty are kept here under lock and key.

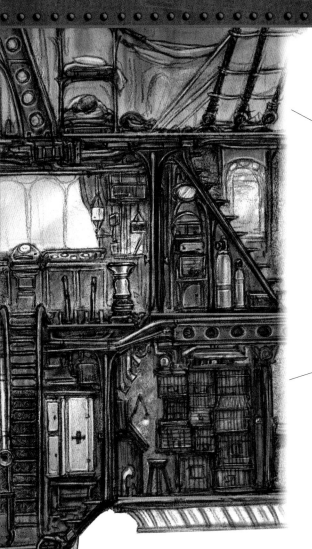

Riggers' Quarters

The riggers sleep on the top deck of the gondola, near their stations on the topside. The riggers' most important job is to maintain the harness, the giant girdle of ropes and ratlines that binds the gondola to the airbeast.

Lizard Room

This is where the *Leviathan*'s boffin of message lizards directs communication through the ship, preventing traffic jams and prioritizing important messages. Lizards are also treated here when they get sick. It's often said that a ship without healthy message lizards will soon find itself in chaos.

Recon Bell

This small spherical room is for taking sightings useful for navigation, reconnaissance, and bombing attacks. The large device is an aerial camera, and the smaller one is the ship's bombsight, used to guide the ship's aerial bombs to their targets. Both devices can be used to help determine the *Leviathan*'s ground speed and position.

The Bridge

From the bridge the captain and his officers send out commands to every part of the ship—to the engines, the rookery, the bomb bay, even to the crewmen on the topside. Most of these orders travel by message lizard, but some parts of the ship are linked by speaking tubes or fabricated nervous tissue, and sometimes a messenger bird is sent the length of the ship.

MASTER WHEEL
This sends signals to the other end of the ship, where giant rudders nudge the ship into turns. But as with riding a horse, the airbeast ultimately decides where it wants to go. The captain can only prod it one way or another.

CODING TABLE
Here the ship's cryptologist decodes secret orders from the Admiralty or semaphore messages from other ships.

SPEAKING TUBES
Several speaking tubes carry officers' commands straight to the navigators' room, the recon bell, and the lizard room, all of which are directly below the bridge.

AVIARY
This cage is stocked with well-rested messenger birds at all times. Birds bringing messages to the ship are trained to land here.

The Rookery

The rookery is where the *Leviathan*'s war birds are kept. Flocks of strafing hawks, fighting eagles, and messenger birds live in nine large cages, which can be opened directly into the air. The rookery is a noisy place and smells of bird clart, so it's well separated from the gondola. The cages are big enough for the rook men to enter and outfit the beasties for battle and with message tubes.

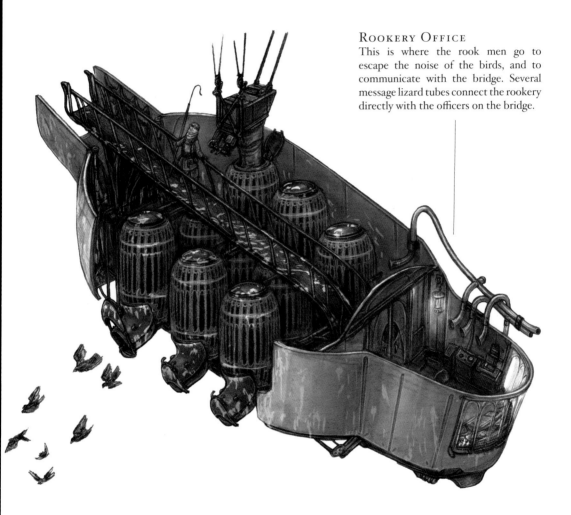

ROOKERY OFFICE
This is where the rook men go to escape the noise of the birds, and to communicate with the bridge. Several message lizard tubes connect the rookery directly with the officers on the bridge.

Beasties

In Darwinist cultures fabricated animals take the place of machines and other technologies. They are created from the "life threads" of natural animals, and combine features of various beasts to create new species.

Communication Beasties

Confingo sterna viator

MESSENGER TERN

The Air Service messenger tern is based on the life threads of the greater crested tern, a seabird of the great southern oceans. Messenger terns can fly thousands of miles, feeding on fish by diving into the water. (The message tube is waterproof, of course.) Note that this creature's legs are derived from the life threads of the Indian giant squirrel. A true chimera!

Remember, I mimic your tone, so always dictate as though you were addressing an officer.

Confingo callisaurus ethologus

Message Lizard

The humble message lizard is used throughout Darwinist culture—not only in military service, but also for business missives and for summoning servants in better households. Its ability to mimic any sound or voice, and to stick to any surface as it scampers along, makes it useful in every situation. The message lizard delivers its messages as a parrot would, imitating the voice and cadence of the sender. Each beast is branded with an identification number to make message trafficking simpler.

Confingo cheiromeles contendo

FLÉCHETTE BATS

"Fléchette" is the French word for "dart." These bats are designed to ingest steel spikes in their food and then release them over the enemy. They are trained to expel the darts when a red light is shone upon the bats, which allows for exact targeting. Fléchette bat attacks are best undertaken at night, when the darkness provides contrast for the spotlight's color.

Confingo accipiter conseco

STRAFING HAWK

"Strafe" comes from the German word for "punishment," and strafing hawks have two ways of delivering punishment to Britain's enemies. They can be equipped with nets made of acid-filled spider silk to slice Clanker aeroplanes apart, or fitted with steel talons for attacking zeppelins or infantry. The beast shown here is equipped with both weapons, though in practice only one at a time can be carried.

Naval Beasties

The Behemoth

The behemoth is a singular creature originally fabricated for the sultan of the Ottoman Empire. It was, however, seized at the start of the war to prevent it from falling into Clanker hands. A thousand feet long, the behemoth has tentacles like a kraken's but also has a massive body covered with bony armored plates. The behemoth has a huge maw and is capable of swallowing a smaller enemy warship or drawing a larger one down beneath the waves. The behemoth is derived from the life threads of the long-armed squid, the sandal-eyed squid, and the pelican eel.

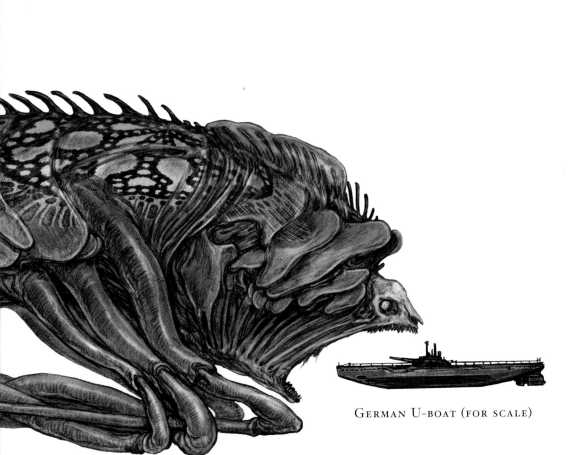

GERMAN U-BOAT (FOR SCALE)

KRAKENS

The kraken is the backbone of the Royal Navy and is large enough to pull an entire ship beneath the waves. Krakens are guided to their targets by spotlights, either from seagoing ships or from airships, and therefore work best at night. They are fabricated from the life threads of the giant squid.

Beasts of the Czar's Armies

FIGHTING BEARS

Russian fighting bears are famous for their ferocity and strength. As tall as a house, they can carry riflemen or cargo at speeds of up to forty miles an hour. When charging the enemy in combat, they engage with claws and teeth while their riflemen fire down from above. Fighting bears are difficult to handle, however, and once out of control can turn on their own crewmen without mercy.

LUPINE TIGERESQUE

This cross between an extinct tiger and a Russian steppe wolf was developed by the tsar's boffins but is used by the British armed forces as well. Though not as formidable as a fighting bear, it is much easier to train and control.

Beasts of Burden

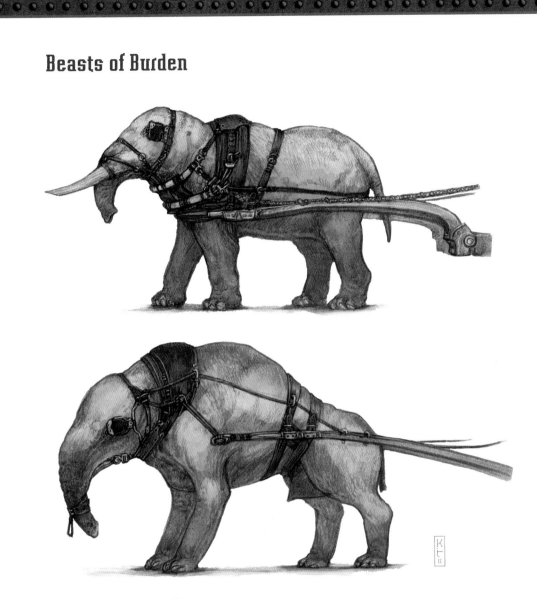

MAMMOTHINES AND ELEPHANTINES

The Darwinist powers' heavy cargo is usually carried by elephantines, created from the life threads of African elephants. In colder regions such as Russia, mammothines are used. Like the lupine tigeresque, which was created partly from the life threads of the extinct saber-toothed tiger, mammoths were a prehistoric creature brought back to serve mankind. The czar of Russia himself travels in an opulent house carried by two mammothines, though more humble passenger contrivances are often used as well.

Other Beasties

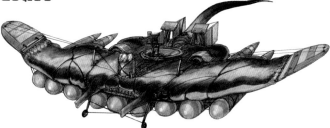

Manta Cutter

Combatants in the Mexican Revolution are supplied by both Darwinist and Clanker powers, and the manta ship is an example of how these technologies mix. The airbeast forms the control surface, instinctively gliding the craft through the air like a fish through water, while Clanker hydrogen cells and engines keep it aloft. The barbed tail is a deadly weapon when the creature is angry.

Fighting Bulls

Fabricated bulls can stand fifteen feet tall, weigh many times more than their natural cousins, and carry crews of two or three men. Receiving a charge from such creatures will test the mettle of even the most disciplined enemy.

Kappa

Based on a mythical water spirit, these deadly creatures were fabricated by the Japanese navy. Kappa are undetectable underwater, but when they leap through the water's surface and onto an enemy ship's decks, they can strip a vessel of its crew in minutes, crushing most crewmen instantly but hauling many back into the ocean for a later repast.

Nycticebus perscitus

THE PERSPICACIOUS LORIS

Talking fabricated creatures, such as the message lizard or the parrot dragon, have long been known to blurt out unexpected words at odd times. Strangely, these utterances sometimes seem . . . perspicacious. In 1910 a small team of boffins lead by Dr. Nora Barlow began to breed for exactly this characteristic—a tendency to say useful things—and the result was the perspicacious loris. Whether this experiment flies in the face of the First Law of Darwinism, "Thou shalt fabricate no beast with reason," is still a matter of furious debate. The lorises certainly can be amusing, though.

HUXLEY ASCENDER

The Huxley, the first hydrogen breather ever fabricated, is named after Darwin's great ally Thomas Henry Huxley, a pugnacious champion of the theory of natural selection and an expert on medusae (jellyfish), from which the ascender is derived. Easy to breed and hard to kill, the Huxley is still in wide use in the empire, despite its nervous disposition. Carrying a crew of one, a Huxley is used for reconnaissance, training, and swift descents from airships. They are considered too dangerous for civilian use.

On the adjoining page is the Huxley Semaphore, a form of semaphore adapted for Huxley scouts.

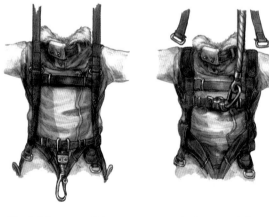

The "sliding escape" is a means to reach the ground from a Huxley as quickly as possible, by reconfiguring the pilot's harness and using it to slide down the line that tethers the Huxley to the ground. It is extremely dangerous and is recommended only in emergencies.

All able bodied seamen are recommended to keep reference cards on their person until the information covered is second nature.

Uniforms Aboard the *Leviathan*

TOPSIDE

When topside in the cold, all crewmen and officers wear fur-lined leather uniforms with safety harnesses. Riggers wear fur at all times, as do fabricant men, who take care of animals on the topside. Note the air rifle, which creates no spark and is too quiet to scare any nervous beasties.

Fabricant Man   Apprentice Rigger   Engine Man   Rigger

SAILORS

When on duty in the gondola, sailors and engineers wear white uniforms and are distinguishable only by their shoulder patches. Note that all rank insignias contain the nautilus, the symbol of Darwinist fabrication.

Bosun   Chief Engineer   Chief of Fabricants   Sailor

Midshipman

Flight Sublieutenant

Flight Lieutenant

Squadron Leader

Brass

Flight Captain

Air Marshal

OFFICERS

All officers wear jackets and ties when on duty in the gondola, and are distinguished by braid on their sleeves rather than shoulder patches. The uniforms shown are normal duty dress; formal dress uniforms include tailcoats and bow ties.

Clanker Uniforms

An officer of the Hapsburg Armor Corps. The spiked *pickelhaube* helmet is usually removed inside walkers.

The Armor Corps uses a curved saber, suitable for both dueling and a cavalry charge.

An officer of the Hapsburg House Guard cavalry. The flat-topped *pickelhaube* helmet is called a *tschapka* and denotes a cavalry unit that uses lances as well as swords.

Crewmen of the Hapsburg Armor Corps.
A metal mask provides protection for
looking out viewing slits during combat.

The padded thigh guards protect the
wearer during a bumpy ride or a crash.
Gunners in a walker's belly also appreciate
the protection when crouching with their
knees against hard metal.

The Clankers

Rising up to contest the Darwinist Powers are those countries who reject the principles of animal fabrication. These so-called Clanker countries prefer their machines to be made of metal, not living tissue. Standing at the heart of this alliance is the German Empire. Its ruler, Kaiser Wilhelm II, has worked to link Clankers everywhere with huffing trains and steamships, and has sent his engineers across the globe to spread the word that diesel engines are superior to sinews and beating hearts. His old ally Austria-Hungary has fallen into line, and lands as widely spread as Japan and the northern United States have adopted Clanker technologies.

Cyklop Stormwalker

The Stormwalker is the smallest two-legged combat walker in the Austrian army. Lightly armed but capable of reaching speeds of sixty kilometers per hour, it is used for scouting and surprise attacks but rarely in intense battles, where they have a tendency to be knocked over. It is not used for long missions, as the cabins are extremely small and uncomfortable.

The Stormwalker's controls are difficult to master, requiring coordination between the pilot's hands and feet to make the machine walk properly. The key elements of the control panel are labeled below.

HAND THROTTLE

KNEE PRESSURE GAUGE

FUEL PUMP CONTROLS

HAND WINCH

HORN SWITCH

CONTROL SAUNTERS (IN HANDS)

EMERGENCY ENGINE SHUTDOWN LEVER

The standard Austrian army version of the Stormwalker is shown above, and the Hapsburg House Guard version, tasked with defending members of the Austrian royal family, below.

ENGINES

The Stormwalker is powered by two Daimler engines, each producing 140 horsepower. The entire machine weighs thirty-five tons.

FUEL TANKS

The Stormwalker's fuel tanks are mounted outside the main armor. This makes them more vulnerable to enemy fire, but also gives the crew a greater chance of survival should the tanks burst into flame.

Stormwalker Cutaway

PILOT'S CABIN
The upper cabin houses a commander, a pilot, and a machine gunner. The commander often sticks his head out of the top hatch and gives commands by tapping his feet on the pilot's shoulders. The grilled viewing port (cut away here) can be opened or closed, depending on conditions. Because piloting with an open viewport in battle conditions can be hazardous, the machine gunner is typically also trained as a spare pilot.

GUNNER'S CABIN
The lower cabin is crewed by a gunner and a loader, the latter doubling as the walker's mechanic. The walker's primary gun is a 57-millimeter cannon that fires 3-kilogram shells. The Stormwalker is entered through a hatchway in the belly of this cabin.

MACHINE GUNS
Two Spandau MG08 machine guns are mounted in the pilot's cabin, one on either side. In practice, however, only one can be fired at a time, and doing so fills the cabin with smoke, noise, and flying cartridges.

Walkers of the Ottoman Empire

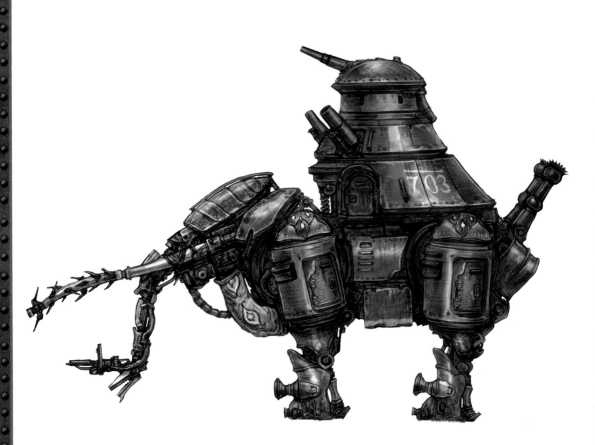

The Sultan's Elephants

The power of the Sultan resides in his army of war elephants. Each weighs 150 tons and has a crew of twenty, including a driver for each leg. The turret holds a cannon and two mortars, and the trunk is tipped with a machine gun.

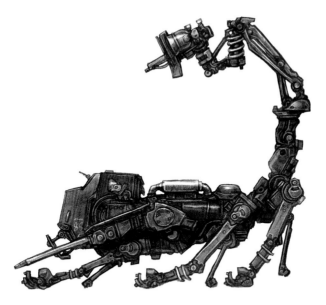

Sand Devil

These scorpion-shaped walkers patrol the beaches of the Ottoman Empire. With an array of spotlights and a machine gun in their tails, they defend the empire against invaders from the sea.

Draft Animals

Most Ottoman walkers take the shapes of animals or mythical creatures. Even the humble donkey, camel, and water buffalo serve as models for Ottoman mechaniks.

The Walkers of Istanbul's Ghettos

The people of Istanbul are divided into many religions, languages, and nationalities. Each group builds their own walkers, all in different shapes. By law, however, only the sultan's walkers may be armed, so the others use fists, blades, or clubs to fight. They are used in parades, in religious ceremonies, and in ritual combat to settle scores between the city's various ethnicities.

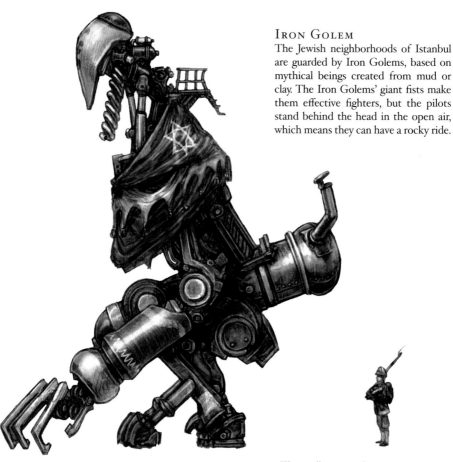

Iron Golem

The Jewish neighborhoods of Istanbul are guarded by Iron Golems, based on mythical beings created from mud or clay. The Iron Golems' giant fists make them effective fighters, but the pilots stand behind the head in the open air, which means they can have a rocky ride.

The walkers on these two pages and pages 38–39 are all shown in scale with this soldier.

ŞAHMERAN

The Kurdish people build their walkers in the shape of Şahmeran, a mythical snake goddess. These machines don't really walk but slide along the ground, thanks to an array of "feet" on their bellies. They can rise up (as shown) or lie flat like a snake for faster movement.

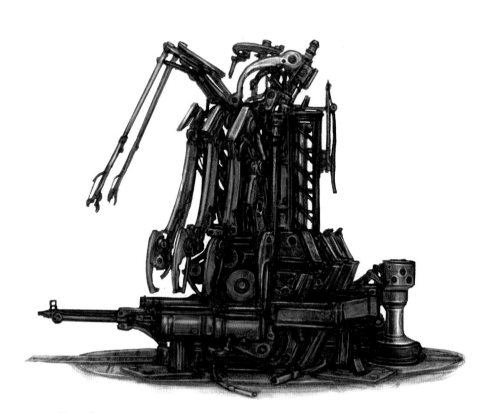

THE SPIDER

It is often said that the various factions in the Ottoman Revolution were woven together by a printing press. This eight-armed press handled all steps of the printing and binding process, and helped spread the revolutionaries' propaganda throughout the empire.

SCARABS

The walking taxicabs of Istanbul are in the shapes of scarab beetles, which are sacred in Egyptian mythology.

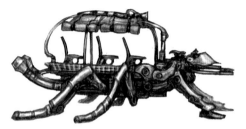

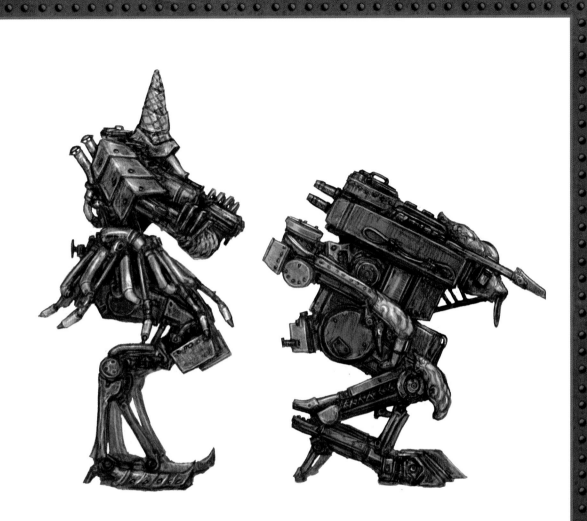

Djinn

Arabs in the Ottoman Empire use walkers in the shapes of the djinn, magical creatures that are often called "genies." These walkers sport skirts of steam cannon, which allow them to disappear behind giant clouds of hot vapor. This gives them a significant advantage on windless days. Djinn pilots are trained to fight while temporarily blinded by steam clouds.

Minotaur

The Greek citizens of Istanbul build walkers in the shapes of the Minotaur, a half-bull, half-man creature of mythology. The Minotaur fights by charging its opponents and impaling them with the spearlike "horn" mounted on its head.

Camera Walkers

Since the motion picture craze began, many walkers have been built to carry cameras instead of weapons. The six legs on this Hearst-Pathé walker keep the camera steady, to prevent motion sickness in moviegoers.

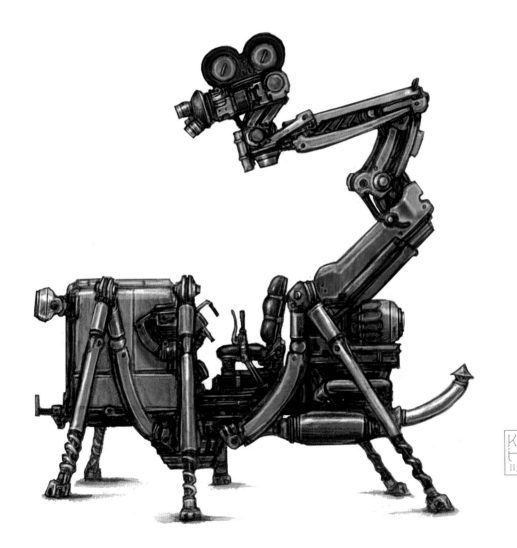

PINKERTON WALKER

The Pinkerton Detective Agency has several small walkers that can be hired for private security. Though only lightly armed and armored, they are the closest thing to a military walker that an individual civilian can obtain. They are expensive, however, renting for as much as seventy U.S. dollars a day, crew included.

This camera walker, used by the revolutionary army of Pancho Villa, was built from the parts of several destroyed German combat walkers. It was affectionately known as *"El Pollo Grande."*

Water-Walkers

Wasser-wanderers are the result of a German secret program to create walkers that can walk fully submerged. These walkers are carried across the water by transport ships to twenty miles from shore and are then lowered onto the ocean floor to begin in secrecy their approach to their target. They can be detected, however, by the trail of exhaust bubbles in their wake.

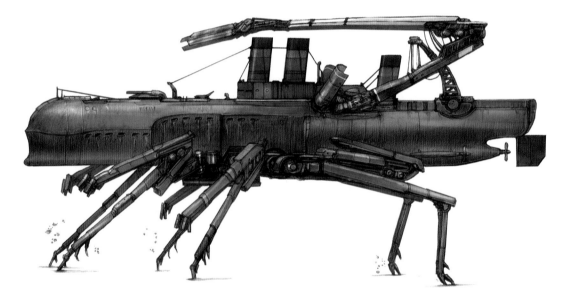

SEAWOLF-CLASS FRIGATE
The largest of the water-walkers is the Seawolf (*Seewolf*). Designed as a raider, it is armed with one 88-millimeter cannon and relies mostly on surprise in its coastal attacks. It also has a pair of kraken-fighting arms, in case it encounters Darwinist beasts in the deep.

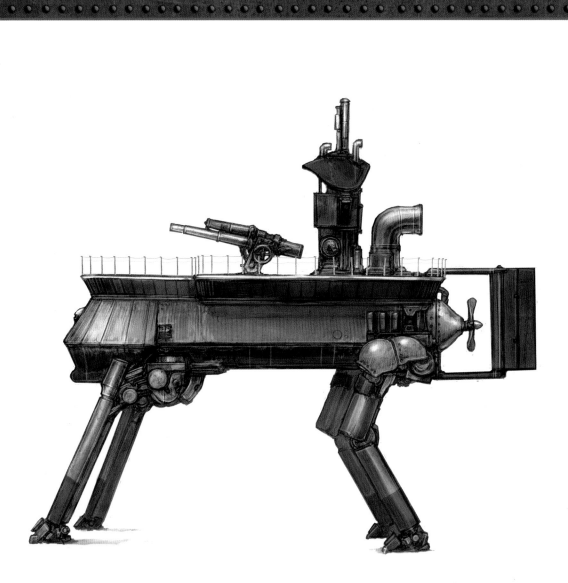

OTTER-CLASS CORVETTE
These smaller walkers serve as escorts for the Seawolves, scouting ahead to check the terrain of the ocean floor and to set off any underwater mines. The Otter carries a single 57-millimeter cannon.

The *Goeben*

Launched in 1911, the S.M.S. *Goeben* was the first German battle cruiser armed with a Tesla cannon, and it had its own gyrothopter and even a detachable U-boat. Since the *Goeben* was trapped in the Mediterranean when the Great War began, the Germans gave the cruiser to the sultan to lure the Ottomans to the Clanker side. She served as the flagship of the Ottoman navy for only a month before being sunk by the behemoth within sight of Istanbul.

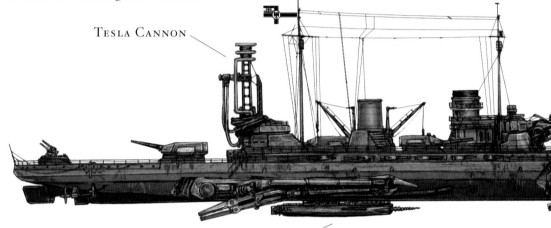

TESLA CANNON

DETACHABLE U-BOAT WITH SCREW RAM

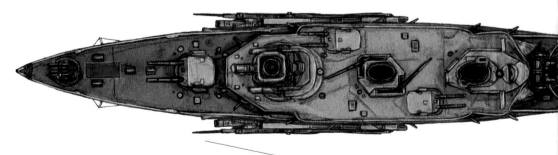

AFT KRAKEN-FIGHTING ARMS

Vital Statistics

ARMAMENT: *8 11-inch guns on four turrets*
LENGTH: *612 feet*
WEIGHT: *24,000 tons*
COMPLEMENT: *43 officers; 1,010 men*

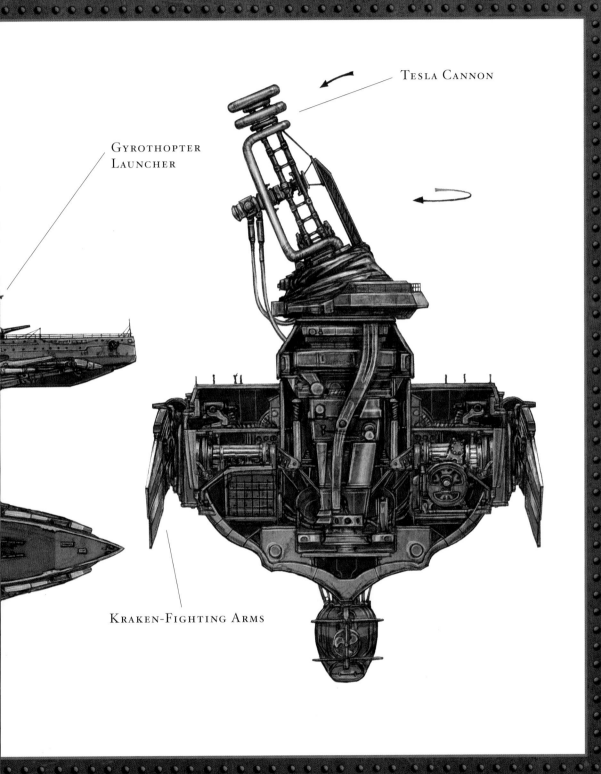

TESLA CANNON

GYROTHOPTER
LAUNCHER

KRAKEN-FIGHTING ARMS

The Orient-Express

This famous train links Berlin and Istanbul. It carries passengers in luxury, and military supplies in secret compartments. Its huge arms can unload cargo, refuel the coal engines, or even fight off attacking bandits if need be. It is said that at night the head of the Express's engine looks like a steam-hissing one-eyed dragon.

Clanker Aircraft

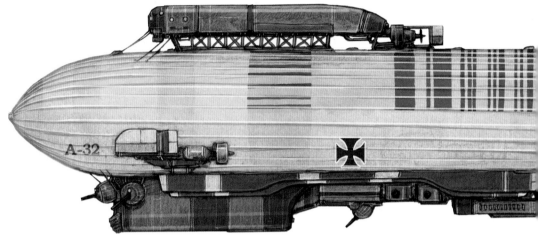

ZEPPELIN CONDOR Z-50

A small Clanker airship used to deliver ground troops into battle. Armed only with machine guns, the Condor carries fifty specially trained commandoes, who slide down rope lines from a height of ten to twenty meters. The commandoes are armed with rifles and anti-walker cannon, which are assembled on the ground.

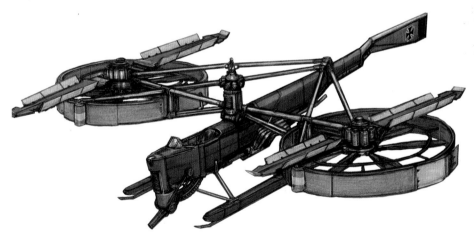

GYROTHOPTER

A one-man aircraft with a pair of rotary wings, designed to take off from ships in the German navy. Gyrothopters can't stay in the air long or carry much cargo, and are generally unarmed except for light munitions such as fireworks. They are mostly used to spot for the ship's guns or in a scouting role.

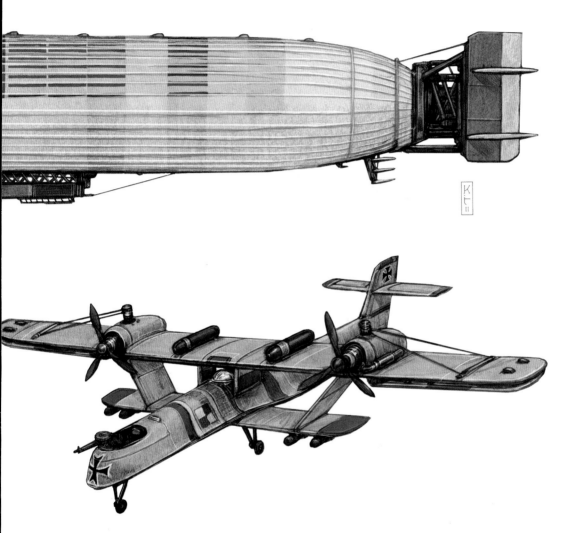

Fokker M Monoplane

One of the first two-seater German aeroplanes with a single wing. The gunner sat in the forward position and the pilot behind. These planes could fly as high as an airship, and a squadron of them was credited with shooting down the H.M.S. *Leviathan* in the early hours of the Great War. None of the aeroplanes survived, however, so the battle could be called a draw.

PRINCE ALEKSANDAR OF HOHENBERG is the only child of the murdered Archduke Franz Ferdinand of Austria. Unable to inherit his father's title, Prince Alek worked with Darwinist forces to help end the Great War. He is now an honorary director of the London Zoological Society.

Midshipman Dylan Sharp served aboard the H.M.S. *Leviathan* during the Great War. Forming a lasting friendship with Prince Aleksandar, he is credited with helping the young prince see the advantages of Darwinism, and is also now in the employ of the London Zoological Society.

WILDCOUNT ERNST VOLGER of Austria was the closest friend of Archduke Ferdinand, and he spent the Great War mentoring the late archduke's son in the arts of international diplomacy. He is currently working to preserve wild fauna in his native lands against the encroachment of fabricated invader species.

Dr. Emma Nora Barlow, née Darwin, furthered her grandfather's work in the field of airbeast fabrication, but she is most famous for her work with talking animals such as the message parrot and the perspicacious loris. Her current position is director of the London Zoological Society.

Coexistence